For Freya

This book is dedicated to the disappearing apple orchards of England

Requests for permission to make copies of any part of the work should be mailed to:
Permissions Department, Harcourt Brace & Company, 6277 Sea Harbor Drive,
Orlando, Florida 32887-6777.

First U.S. edition 1996
First published in Great Britain in 1996 by Andersen Press Ltd.

Library of Congress Cataloging-in-Publication Data
Nightingale, Sandy.
Cider apples/written and illustrated by Sandy Nightingale.
p. cm.
Summary: At the magical moment between the old year
and the new, a young girl and her grandmother enlist the aid of some
fairies to save their apple trees.
ISBN 0-15-201244-3
[1. Magic—Fiction. 2. Fairies—Fiction. 3. Apples—Fiction.
4. Grandmothers—Fiction.] I. Title.
PZ7.N5845Ci 1996
[E]—dc20 95-49311

A C E F D B

Printed in Italy

Cider Apples

WRITTEN AND ILLUSTRATED BY

Sandy Nightingale

Harcourt Brace & Company

SAN D... ...NDON

It was just before midnight on New Year's Eve. Holly couldn't sleep. She could hear her grandparents talking in the sitting room below.

"There's nothing we can do." That was Grandpa's voice. "The apple trees are dying, and if they die we will have to sell the cottage."

"Something may turn up," said Grandma.

"I don't think so," said Grandpa. "We can't manage without the cider-apple money."

Holly caught her breath. Grandpa's grandpa had lived in this cottage and Holly loved coming to stay here.

After Grandpa had gone to bed, Holly ran downstairs.

"Oh, Grandma," she cried, "you can't sell Apple
Tree Cottage."

"Cheer up," smiled Grandma. "I haven't given
up hope. New Year is such a magical time, anything
might happen. Just wait and see."

Just then, the clock on the mantelpiece chimed the
first stroke of midnight.

"At last!" purred a strange musical voice. It
was Magic the cat. Holly and Grandma stared in
amazement.

"Come on!" said Magic. "There's no time to lose."

He looked at their wondering faces.

"Animals can speak in the moments between the old year and the new," he explained. "Shadow has something important to tell you."

In his stable, Shadow tossed his mane.

"When I was a foal," he began, "I heard a strange tale about the apple tree man who looks after orchards. Listen carefully. This is what you must do if you want to save the apple trees . . ."

"Take the last drop of last year's cider and put it
into a big pan with some cinnamon and honey.
Heat it gently. Pour the warm cider over the roots of
the oldest tree in the orchard and see what happens.
But hurry! The magic only works tonight."

Holly and Grandma did exactly as Shadow told them.

As soon as the cider soaked into the frozen ground,
a ring of toadstools sprang out of the snow.

"Stand back," whispered Grandma. "You must
never step inside a fairy ring."

For a moment everything was silent.

Then, suddenly, there appeared from the roots of the tree a stream of fairies, laughing, singing, and dancing. They poured into the orchard, flew up into the branches, and tumbled into the air. Some played musical instruments, strumming, piping, and beating time as they whirled around.

Holly watched with shining eyes. She had never seen anything so beautiful.

A peculiar old man was grinning at them from the tree. He clapped his long, bony hands, and the fairies were quiet.

"I know why you have called me here." He laughed. "But I can only heal these trees if Holly will promise to plant all the seeds from the first apple she picks."

He looked at Holly. "Will you promise me this?"

"Oh, I promise!" Holly cried.

The apple tree man nodded his head and clapped his hands again. The fairy music became louder and louder as a troupe of fairies moved through the orchard, dancing around every tree.

Then, just as suddenly as they had come, the fairies disappeared.

Holly and Grandma gazed around the quiet orchard.
Everything was still.

"Let's get you tucked into bed," said Grandma.
"It's freezing. We've done what we can. Now we
must wait."

Holly climbed into her cozy bed and fell asleep
at once. Outside, the snow began to fall silently.

A robin singing outside the window woke Holly.
She remembered the orchard. She ran to the
window and looked out at the snowy world. Did
the trees look any different?

Grandma woke with the wintry sunshine streaming
into the bedroom. She stretched and yawned.

"I've had such a funny dream," she said. Then
she heard Holly calling.

"Grandma, Grandpa, come and look! Come
and see!"

Out in the orchard, covered with snow, the oldest
tree was laden with perfect, juicy apples. Grandpa
stared in wonder.

"It's a miracle," he said. "Our house is saved."

Holly ran to the tree.

Shadow deserves an apple, she thought.

"Thank you, Apple Tree Man," she whispered.
"I won't forget my promise." And she reached up
to pick her first apple.